Read With Me

STORYTIME

BRIMAX

First published in 2001 by Brimax
an imprint of Octopus Publishing Group Ltd
2-4 Heron Quays, London, E14 4JP
© Octopus Publishing Group Ltd
Printed in Spain

CONTENTS

TEDDY TALES

Teddy and the Ghost

Teddy was bored.
"I know," said Teddy. "I'll make
some mud castles in the garden."
Teddy made four mud castles.
Then he built a wall joining them
all together. He dug a moat and
then he poured water into it.
Teddy collected lots of pebbles
and stuck them to the castle walls.

Teddy was very pleased with himself. Then just as he turned to go inside, he saw it. A ghost! It was big and white and drifting across the grass. Teddy could see two dark patches that looked like eyes! Teddy was scared.

"AAAGH!" cried Teddy as he ran into the house. "Dad! Dad!" he yelled.

Father Bear was nowhere to be found. Teddy ran back into the kitchen. Through the window he saw something strange. Father Bear was running around the garden. Teddy forgot how frightened he was and peeped around the kitchen door. Father Bear was chasing the ghost! Round the garden he ran, trying to catch it. But every time he came close to it, the ghost drifted off.

Just then Father Bear saw Teddy.
"Help me, Teddy!" he yelled. "The
wind is blowing the sheets away
and they're getting muddy!"
The ghost was really a sheet!
That evening when Teddy went to
bed he was still giggling. But in the
night he was woken by a strange
sound: "Woooo! Woooo!"
"It's only the wind," said Teddy.
But he was never really sure...

Teddy Falls in Love

A new family of bears had moved next door to Teddy. Mirabelle Bear was the same age as Teddy. Teddy liked Mirabelle straight away. Soon Teddy found himself thinking about her all the time.

"I must love Mirabelle," said Teddy to Mother Bear one day. "If I love her, I should marry her."

"You're too young to get married," said Mother Bear.

"I'll wait until I'm old enough," said Teddy. "I'll send her a Valentine's Day card and ask her to wait, too." Teddy began making his card. He drew hearts and flowers and painted them brightly. When the card was finished, Teddy wrote a message inside. It said: 'Dear Mirabelle, I would like to marry you when I'm old enough, so please wait. Love from T'.

On Valentine's Day, Teddy got up early to deliver his card. He took an orange to eat on the way. As Teddy walked along, he saw Mirabelle! Mirabelle smiled. Teddy grinned back. As he did, the juice from his orange squirted out of his mouth and dribbled down his chin! Mirabelle laughed. Teddy felt very silly. He ran all the way home.

Teddy hid in his bedroom. He would have stayed there all day but Father Bear called him downstairs. A card had been delivered for him. Teddy opened it. A huge smile spread across his face. On the front of the card were hearts and flowers, and the words inside said: 'Dear Teddy, I would like to marry you when I'm old enough, so please wait. Love from M'.

Can you find five differences between these two pictures?

What is Teddy doing?

digging

drawing

running

smiling

Teddy Race Activity

Teddy and Father Bear chased after the flyaway sheet. Guess who reached the sheet in the shortest time? Adding the seconds as you go, trace along the tangled lines to see if you are right.

Father Bear

Teddy Bear

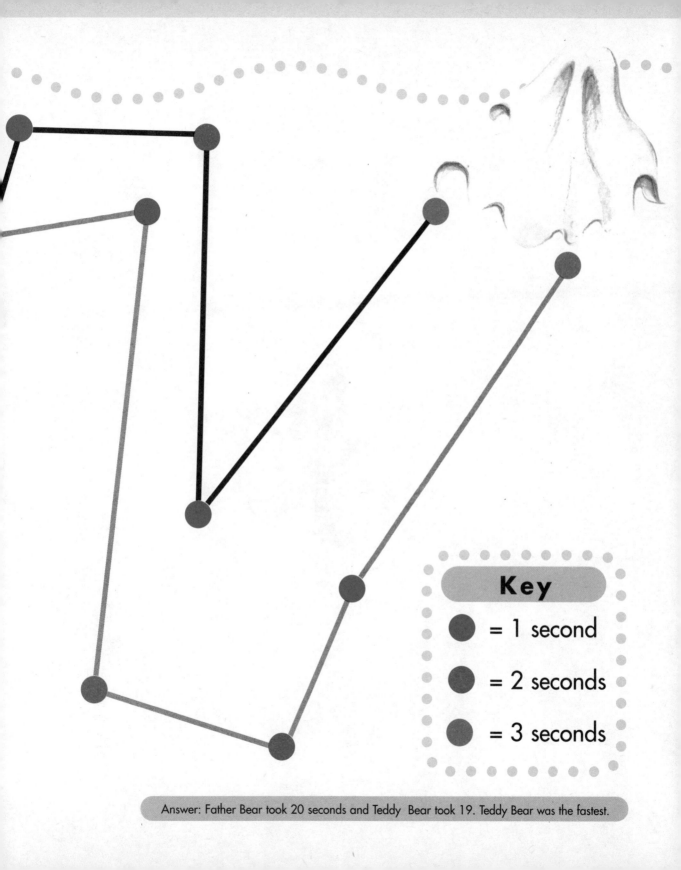

Key

● = 1 second

● = 2 seconds

● = 3 seconds

Answer: Father Bear took 20 seconds and Teddy Bear took 19. Teddy Bear was the fastest.

TEDDY AND THE BEANSTALK

Teddy and the Beanstalk

It was lunchtime. Teddy looked at
his plate. "Where do beans come
from?" he asked Mother Bear.
"They grow," said Mother Bear.
"How do they grow?" asked Teddy.
"I'll show you," said Mother Bear.
She filled a plant pot with soil. Then
she planted a bean. She watered
the pot and put it in a sunny spot in
the garden.

"A beanstalk will grow. The beans come from the beanstalk," said Mother Bear.

"What if I want an orange?" asked Teddy.

"Then you must plant an orange seed," said Mother Bear.

"What I plant is what will grow!" said Teddy. He filled a pot with soil. Then Teddy took something from his pocket and planted it in the soil. He watered the pot and put it in the sun.

The following week Teddy and Mother Bear looked in their pots. In Mother Bear's pot, they saw a small, green shoot. But in Teddy's pot, they saw a large, pink shoot!

"What did you plant in your pot, Teddy?" gasped Mother Bear.

"A jellybean!" said Teddy with a grin.

"You are silly!" laughed Mother Bear.

Teddy and the Play

Teddy heard the door bell ring.
Mouse, Squirrel and Rabbit were
standing on the doorstep.
"Hello, Teddy," said Mouse. "It's my
Dad's birthday on Sunday and
we're going to put on a play for him
in the school hall. Will you be in it?"
"Oh, yes please!" said Teddy. He
hoped he might be given the most
important part in the play. After all,
he was the biggest.

"We want you to be a tree," said Mouse.

"A tree?" said Teddy in surprise.

"Yes, Rabbit will hide behind you," said Mouse.

Teddy decided to be the best tree ever seen in a play. He put on his brown jeans to look like a tree trunk, and his green sweatshirt to look like leaves. He stood with his arms in the air like branches.

By Sunday Teddy had a cold. It was too late to find someone else to be the tree. Mouse and Squirrel stuck leaves and twigs to Teddy to make him look like a real tree. Now all the grown-ups were arriving at the hall. Teddy went to his place on the stage and became a tree. Teddy's friends started to act out the play. They were just getting to the most exciting part when the 'tree' felt a tickle in his nose. "AAAATISHOO!" sneezed the tree.

It was such a big sneeze that poor
Rabbit was knocked off his feet.
He picked himself up and brushed
leaves and twigs from his head.
He started to say his next line but
no one heard it.

"AAAATISHOO!" sneezed the tree
again. Teddy felt miserable. He was
ruining the play and Mouse would
be sad.

The friends carried on, but they had to shout their lines! When the play was finished, Father Mouse wiped tears of laughter from his eyes. "That was the best birthday present I've ever had," he said. "The play was very good. I liked the sneezing tree. Whose idea was that?"

Can you find five differences between these two pictures?

What is Teddy doing?

eating

planting

smiling

sneezing

Teddy Fishing Activity

"Have you caught anything with your little fishing rod?" Teddy Bear asked Rabbit one day.

S   **F**   **H**   **I**

1
2
3
4

"Yes!" smiled Rabbit. "Starting at number **1**, trace along all four tangled fishing lines. The letters at the end will tell you what I've caught!"

Answer: FISH

TEDDY'S LOST TOY

Teddy's Lost Toy

Teddy was glad to be going to
Grandma's house for the day.
Mother Bear was spring-cleaning
Teddy was bored. He sat on the
doorstep waiting for Grandma to
arrive. Suddenly there was a shout
from upstairs.
"Teddy! Come quickly!" cried
Mother Bear.

Teddy went upstairs to his bedroom. "Look what I've found!" said Mother Bear, holding up a small, dusty, cuddly toy that didn't look like anything at all. "It's Thing!" "THING!" cried Teddy joyfully. "You've been found at last!" And he hugged the long lost toy and danced around the room with it. "Oh, Thing!" said Teddy. "I promise never to lose you again..." He was interrupted by Grandma knocking at the door.

Teddy put his toy on his pillow. Because he was sad to leave it behind, he picked it up again. He put it down and then picked it up, put it down and then picked it up until Mother Bear told him to hurry. Teddy ran downstairs. Grandma helped him into her car and they drove off. Teddy loved visiting Grandma and they had a big lunch at her house followed by ice cream for dessert. Then they went to the park to play and stopped for hotdogs on the way home.

When they arrived home, Teddy saw that something was wrong.
The house was a terrible mess.
Teddy's friends were there too.
They seemed to be looking for something.
"What's going on?" Teddy asked Mother Bear.
"Poor Teddy," she said. "I don't know how to tell you this... Thing is lost again."
Teddy gulped.
"I noticed he was missing after you left. I must have put him somewhere..." said Mother Bear.

"We've looked everywhere," said Teddy's friend Squirrel.
"Even in the garden," said Rabbit. Everyone tried to cheer up Teddy. At last Teddy said, "I think this is my fault, you see..." And with that Teddy pulled something small and dusty from his pocket.
"THING!" cried Mother Bear. Everyone started chasing Teddy across the garden. When they caught him, they tickled him until he begged them to stop.

Teddy and the Sea Monster

Waves lapped around Teddy's ankles. The sun was warm on his back. A big smile crept across his face as he gazed out at the sea. "This is the life," he said to himself. Teddy turned to wave to his family, watching him from the beach. Then he turned back to the sea again. And he screamed loudly.

"AAAGH!" cried Teddy, running up the beach as fast as he could.

"What's wrong?" asked Mother Bear.

"A monster in the sea!" gasped Teddy, out of breath.

"A monster?" said Mother Bear.

"Yes! It was HORRIBLE! It had a big, black nose with a hook like an umbrella handle - that's all I could see above the water," said poor Teddy.

"Perhaps I should take a look," said Mother Bear.

"I'll come too," said Grandma, who had been around long enough to see most kinds of monsters.

They walked to the water's edge. Suddenly the monster reared up out of the sea. It *was* horrible! There was the black nose with a hook like an umbrella handle that Teddy had seen. Now he could see its big, glassy eyes, enormous, furry body and webbed feet. It was too scary. Teddy hid his eyes. But Grandma and Mother Bear were laughing. Teddy decided to look with one eye. He did feel silly. The monster was grinning at him. It said, "Hello, Teddy."

"Hello, Dad," said Teddy!

Can you find five differences between these two pictures?

What are they doing?

cleaning

tickling

waving

pointing

Teddy Count Activity

Count how many of each picture there is on the right, then write your answers beside each picture below.

How many can you count?

How many can you count?

How many can you count?

How many can you count?

Answers: There are four bucket pictures, five cars, three pictures of Thing and six toy boxes.

TEDDY'S SHADOW

Teddy's Shadow

It was a sunny day. Teddy was
walking through the meadow.
The sun went behind a cloud.
Teddy saw that his shadow was
gone. After a while he met Rabbit
who was fishing by the lake.
"Have you seen my shadow?"
Teddy asked. "I've lost it!"
"No, Teddy, but I think..." began
Rabbit.

But Teddy ran off, searching for his shadow. Then Teddy passed Squirrel in his garden.

"Have you seen my shadow?" Teddy asked Squirrel. "I've lost it!"

"No I haven't, Teddy, but I think..." began Squirrel.

But Teddy was in too much of a hurry. He ran off, searching for his shadow.

Next Teddy met Mouse who was feeding the ducks.
"Have you seen my shadow?" Teddy asked Mouse. "I've lost it!"
"No I haven't, Teddy, but I think..." began Mouse.
But Teddy was in too much of a hurry. He ran off, searching for his shadow.

Teddy was still searching for his shadow when the sun came out from behind the cloud. Then he noticed his shadow was on the ground again. Just then Rabbit, Squirrel and Mouse caught up with Teddy. Now they could finish telling him what they thought...

"...You'll find your shadow when the sun comes out!" they all said together.

Who will Play with Teddy?

On Teddy's birthday, his Grandma gave him a new kite. When Teddy woke up the next day to find the sun shining, he went to Squirrel's house and knocked on the door. When Squirrel opened the door, Teddy said, "Would you like to come and play with my new kite?" But Squirrel took one look at Teddy, screamed loudly and slammed the door.

So Teddy went to call on Rabbit. But when Rabbit saw Teddy, he screamed loudly and slammed the door, too.

"What is wrong with everyone today?" said Teddy. He decided to try Mouse. He knocked on the door. "Mouse, would you like..." Teddy started to say. But Mouse took one look at Teddy, screamed loudly, and slammed the door.

Teddy began to cry. He walked home all alone.

When Mother Bear saw Teddy coming up the path, she threw her arms in the air.

"Oh, you poor little bear!" she cried. Then she whisked Teddy off to bed.

"What's going on?" asked Teddy. But before Mother Bear could answer, there was a knock at the door.

Teddy could hear his friends talking
to Mother Bear downstairs.
"Have you seen it?" asked Squirrel.
"It's horrible!" said Rabbit.
"A big, spotty monster!" said Mouse.
"You silly animals!" said Mother Bear.
"You haven't seen a monster! That
was Teddy. He has the measles."
Rabbit, Squirrel and Mouse thought
Teddy was a monster because he
was covered in spots. They didn't
mean to be unfriendly. Teddy felt
much better all ready!

Can you find five differences between these two pictures?

What are they doing?

searching

fishing

knocking

crying

Teddy Picture Story Activity

Look at the little pictures opposite. Where do you think each picture should go in the story below?

After eating his breakfast, **1** Teddy

went into the garden. First Teddy did some

digging. **2** Then he did some

planting. **3** As Teddy drew a

picture **4** he began to sneeze. **5**

"Grass always makes me do that!" smiled

Teddy **6** as he ran indoors. **7**

READ WITH ME STORIES

Freddy Fox

"Do you want to go out to play with your friends, Freddy?" asks Freddy's mother.

"I do not want to go out because it is raining," says Freddy.

"Why not?" says Mrs Fox. She is sewing and wants some peace and quiet.

"I do not want to get my tail wet," says Freddy. He is very proud of his beautiful, red tail.

Outside Freddy sees his friend Desmond Duck. Desmond is splashing in the stream.
"Come and play!" he calls.
"I do not want to get my tail wet," calls Freddy.
"If you put your boots on and take an umbrella, you will not get wet," says Mrs Fox.

Freddy goes upstairs to look for his boots and his umbrella.

He looks under the bed. But they are not there. He looks in his wardrobe. But they are not there either.

Freddy hears his mother calling him. "Your boots and your umbrella are down here."

Freddy runs downstairs and is soon ready to go out to play.

Wilbur Weasel comes to play. He shakes his wet fur all over Freddy. "Look out!" shouts Freddy.

"Rain is horrible. What can we do?"

"Lots of things," says Desmond. "First we can play a splashing game. We must find a big puddle, then jump in it as hard as we can. The biggest splash wins!"

Everyone chooses a big puddle and jumps in it as hard as they can. Splash! Desmond makes a big splash. Splash! Wilbur makes a big splash. SPLASH! Freddy makes the biggest splash of all.

"This is fun," says Freddy.

"Excuse me," says a voice from high in the branches of a tree. "I don't think it is fun. You've made my feathers very wet."

Olly Owl flutters his wet wings. "Please stop that at once!" he hoots.

They all scamper away. Freddy's tail is wet at the tip, but he does not notice.

"What shall we do now?" asks Freddy.

"I know," says Wilbur. "We can make some paper boats and sail them along the stream."

The paper boats float along the water.

"We can have a race with the boats," cries Desmond. "Let's go!" The three friends cheer their little boats along the stream. Freddy drops half his tail in the water, but he does not notice - his boat is winning the race! Desmond swims beside the boats. "Look at me," he calls. "I am pretending to be a yellow boat."

"I wish we could all pretend to be boats," says Freddy. Then he has an idea. He takes his umbrella, turns it upside-down and sets it on the water. It floats just like a boat. He jumps into the umbrella. "I am the captain of this boat," he says. Wilbur jumps in beside him. Freddy's tail falls over the side and gets very wet, but he does not notice. He is too busy sailing his umbrella boat.

Then Desmond says, "Time to go home. Come on, everyone." Desmond begins to swim back up the stream. He looks over his shoulder, but Freddy and Wilbur are not behind him. They cannot make the umbrella boat turn around. The stream is carrying them further and further away!

"Help us!" they cry.

Then Mrs Duck swims along. She is looking for Desmond. She sees the umbrella with Freddy and Wilbur in it and quickly swims after it. She pulls it safely to the bank.

"Thank you," gasps Freddy.

He is soaking wet, but he does not notice - he is too busy catching his breath!

Everyone goes back to Freddy's house to dry in front of the fire. Soon, Freddy, Desmond and Wilbur are sitting in front of the fire drinking hot milk and eating cookies. Suddenly Freddy remembers his tail.

"My poor tail," says Freddy.

"You must be very careful when you play near water," scolds Mrs Fox. Mrs Duck has an idea. "I will teach Freddy and Wilbur to swim like ducks," she says. "Then they can play safely in the stream."

"Now, Freddy," says Mrs Fox, "I have a surprise for you. Close your eyes." Freddy closes his eyes.

"Now you can look," says Mrs Fox. She shows Freddy what she has been sewing. It is a bright yellow raincoat!

"You will look just like me," says Desmond.

"I will swim like a duck and look like a duck," laughs Freddy.

Say these words again.

friends	puddle
raining	feathers
beautiful	scamper
stream	sail
winning	yellow
stairs	shoulder
splashing	remembers

What can you see?

tail

umbrella

boots

paper boats

raincoat

Benjamin Rabbit

Benjamin Rabbit is very busy. He and his friends are going to the beach for a picnic, and he is helping to fill the baskets.
Mr Rabbit is making lots of sandwiches and Mrs Rabbit is icing the cake. There are cookies, pies and lemonade. The kitchen is full as everyone helps.

Suddenly they hear a "Toot-toot!" outside. It is Mr Bear, the train driver. He is taking everyone to the beach in his little stream train. "Come along!" he calls. Benjamin's friends are already on the train. Freddy Fox, Billy Bear, Wilbur Weasel, Daisy Dormouse and Desmond Duck are all waiting.

"Wait for me!" cries Benjamin. He runs up with the bulging basket. Mr Bear helps him and the basket onto the train. "Off we go," says Mr Bear. The little train puffs along in the sunshine. Benjamin is sure that this is going to be a special day. The train soon arrives at the beach. "Here we are," says Mr Bear. "Everybody out!"

The sky is blue and the sea is calm. The sand is golden and warm. Benjamin jumps out of the train and pulls off his shoes and his socks. The sand is soft between his toes. "I will race you down to the sea," he calls to his friends, and off they go. Freddy Fox is the winner.

The waves rush up the sand to meet them and Benjamin's toes get wet. "The sea is chasing me," he laughs. They all splash about happily in the water.

Mr Bear is setting out the picnic. "Time for lunch," he calls. Everyone is very hungry. They eat the sandwiches, cake and cookies.

"More lemonade, please," says Benjamin.

"Pass the cookies, please," says Wilbur.

They are all too full to run around anymore!

"What shall we do now?" says Freddy.

"Now we can build a sandcastle," says Benjamin. They decide to make the biggest sandcastle anyone has ever seen.

"We can put all these shells and stones on the sandcastle," says Freddy. They all set to work. The sandcastle grows and grows.

Benjamin goes for a walk along the beach with Daisy and Desmond. They find a sparkling rock pool. In the pool they find a starfish, a jellyfish and long ribbons of seaweed. Benjamin finds lots of shells and smooth, shiny stones. He takes them back to show the others.

Then Benjamin hears a tiny voice calling. It is coming from the sea. "Hello," says the voice.
He goes to see who is there. Swimming about in the waves he see a little mermaid! Her eyes are as blue as the sea. Her hair is as golden as the sand. She has a fish's tail instead of legs.
"Hello," says Benjamin.

"Can you help me please?" says the little mermaid. "I have lost the big, blue stone from my new necklace. The sea has taken it and it must be on the beach. Can you find it for me?"

"We will all look for it," says Benjamin. He tells his friends about the little mermaid's lost stone and everyone starts to search for it.

They all find something. Daisy
finds a starfish. Billy finds a shell.
Wilbur finds a crab. Freddy finds
some seaweed. Desmond finds
a pebble. But no one can find
the mermaid's lost stone.
"Oh dear," says Benjamin. "We
have looked everywhere. Where
can it be?"
Then he sees something shining
on the top of the sandcastle.

"Here is your stone," cries Benjamin. It was on top of the sandcastle the whole time.
The little mermaid is very happy to have her blue stone back.
"Thank you," she says. Now I will give you something." She gives Benjamin a great big sea shell.

"Put it up to your ear," she says.
"I can hear the sea," says
Benjamin in surprise.
"Yes," smiles the mermaid. "Now
you will always be able to hear
the sea, wherever you are."
On the way home, Benjamin
listens to the sea shell. He will
never forget his special day at
the beach.

Say these words again.

picnic	ribbons
sandwiches	around
kitchen	voice
sunshine	instead
golden	blue
special	surprise
sparkling	beach

What can you see?

train

basket

sandcastle

mermaid

blue stone

Gilda the Witch

It is morning in the forest. Gilda the witch turns over in bed. "Time for another little snooze," she says sleepily.

Gilda takes care of the forest with her magic spells. Her cottage is full of magical things. She has a broomstick, a cauldron, a crystal ball and shelves full of books. She also has a cat called Timothy.

Timothy leaps up onto Gilda's bed
and licks the end of her nose.
"What is the matter Timothy?"
mumbles Gilda. "Why are you
waking me up?" She sits up in
bed, and the tip of her witches'
hat falls down over one eye.
"What is that noise?" she
wonders. She hears a strange
noise outside.

Gilda leaps out of bed. Through the window she can see Katie and Bobby Rabbit scampering away in the distance. The sky is blue, the grass is green and the daisies are white and yellow. "How lovely!" sighs Gilda. "Today my spells will sweeten the bees' honey and make the roses smell like perfume."

Gilda is stirring her cauldron when there is a knock at the door. It is Sally Squirrel. "Have you seen what has happened to the forest?" she squeaks. Gilda hurries outside. The trees are as tall as ever. The flowers smell as sweet as ever. Then Gilda sees what is wrong. The sky is not blue. It is green! The grass is not green. It is blue!

"One minute the sky was blue, and now it is green," says Sally. "You must cast a spell to make everything right again." "I need my magic spell book," says Gilda. She hunts along the bookshelves. She hunts under the table. She hunts among the cushions. "Where did I put that spell book?"

Timothy jumps onto the window-sill. He gives a loud meeow. "Are you trying to tell me something?" asks Gilda. Suddenly she remembers what happened that morning, when she heard someone laughing outside the window. Gilda stares at the blue grass and the violet daisies. There are tiny footprints on the grass. "Those look like rabbits' footprints!" she says to herself.

"I know what has happened," Gilda tells Sally. "Someone has taken my spell book and I think I know who. Have you seen Bobby and Katie Rabbit this morning?"

"No," says Sally.

"When we find Bobby and Katie, I think we will find the spell book," says Gilda. "Then we can put everything right again. Come and help me look."

Gilda, Sally and Timothy set out on the trail of the missing spell book. Gilda flies along on her broomstick. Sally jumps from tree to tree. Timothy marches along with his whiskers in the air. They ask everyone they meet if they have seen Bobby and Katie.

"No," says Emma Duckling.

"No," says Hetty Hare.

"No," says Rosie Rabbit.

"No," says George Bear who is busy in his garden. "I hope you find your book soon. I cannot tell my plums from my peaches until everything is put right again." Then Timothy begins to sniff at the bushes. He can hear something. He meeows again. Gilda can hear something too. It sounds just like two little rabbits crying.

"Is that you, Katie and Bobby?" calls Gilda. Katie and Bobby creep out from the bushes. Bobby is carrying Gilda's spell book. "You naughty little rabbits," scolds Gilda. "It was very wrong to take my book without asking." "We are sorry," sniffs Katie. "We only wanted to borrow the book, but we did not want to wake you."

"We wanted to make some magic spells," says Bobby. "We must have mixed them up, because when we said the magic words the sky turned green. And look!" Katie and Bobby turn around. Their tiny tails are not white, but blue! "Never mind, you can help stir the cauldron while I say the spell that will change everything back to normal again," says Gilda.

Everyone goes home to Gilda's cottage. They wait while she finds all the magic things she needs. She needs early morning dew, some moonlight from a silver bottle, some cobwebs, and two hairs from a rabbit's tail.

"It does not matter if they are blue," she says. Then she reads out the magic spell from her book. "Abracadabra!" she cries.

They rush to the window. Gilda's spell has worked! The sky is blue. The grass is green. "Well done," says Sally. "You are a good witch, Gilda." But Katie and Bobby still have their blue tails.

"They will be white again in a few days," Gilda says to them. "That will teach you not to meddle with magic!"

Say these words again.

forest   right
snooze   cushions
magic   laughing
cottage   whiskers
window   suddenly
distance   borrow
sweeten   meddle

What can you see?

broomstick

cauldron

spell book

cat

crystal ball

NOW I CAN READ

Dilly Duck goes to the pond.
Her three little ducklings
go with her.
"Come with me," says Dilly.
"I will take you for a swim
in the duck pond."
But the little ducklings are
afraid. They do not want
to go to the duck pond.
"We do not know how to
swim!" they say.
But Dilly Duck does not
hear them.
Silly Dilly Duck!

Bossy Bear plays with
his roller-skates. He has
a lot of fun.
He sees Dilly Duck come
along the lane. He sees
the three little ducklings
with her.
"Where are you going?"
says Bossy Bear.
"To the duck pond," says the
first little duckling.
"But I do not want to go."

"Why not?" says Bossy Bear.
"I cannot swim," says
the first little duckling.
"We can play a trick," says
Bossy Bear.
"I will go to the duck pond.
You stay here. You can play
with my roller-skates."
The first little duckling
thinks that will be fun.
He puts on the skates.

Dilly Duck is on her way to
have a swim in the duck pond.
The two little ducklings
and Bossy Bear go along too.
But silly Dilly Duck does not
see Bossy Bear.
The two little ducklings and
Bossy Bear think that this
is very funny. Bossy Bear
likes to play funny tricks.

They all go along the lane.
Soon they meet Hoppy Rabbit.
He drives in his little car.
"Where are you going?"
says Hoppy Rabbit.
"To the duck pond," says
the second little duckling.
"But I do not want to go."
"Why not?" says Hoppy.
"I cannot swim," says
the second little duckling.

Hoppy sees Bossy Bear.
"I am a duckling," says Bossy
Hoppy thinks that this is very
funny.
"I will go to the duck pond
too," he says. "Duckling can
drive my car. This is
a very funny trick. Silly
Dilly Duck cannot see us."
The second little duckling
gets into Hoppy's car.

They all go along the lane.
Dilly Duck,
   Bossy Bear,
      Hoppy Rabbit
and one little duckling.
But Dilly Duck does not see
her very funny ducklings.

Soon they meet Paddy Dog.
Paddy Dog plays with his
little red scooter.
"Where are you going?"
says Paddy Dog.
"To the duck pond," says
the third little duckling.
"But I do not want to go."
"Why not?" says Paddy Dog.
"I cannot swim," says
the third little duckling.

Paddy Dog thinks that
this is very funny.
"Bossy and Hoppy are very
funny ducklings," he says.
"I will play a trick too.
Duckling can play with
my little red scooter.
I will be the third
little duckling. Silly
Dilly Duck will not see."

They all go along the lane.
Dilly Duck,
   Bossy Bear,
      Hoppy Rabbit
         and Paddy Dog.
But no little ducklings!
Ozzie Owl is in the old tree.
"Hoo-hoo-hoo!" he hoots.
Cuddly Cat jumps down from
the tree. She thinks they
are all very funny.

At last they come to the pond.
Flippy Frog and Merry Mole
are there. They say,
"What funny ducklings."
Then Dilly Duck sees them.
She is afraid. She looks all
round for her lost ducklings.
And here they come!
One on skates,
   one in the car,
      one on the scooter.

But the little ducklings go
too fast. They cannot stop!
SPLASH! SPLASH! SPLASH!
Three little ducklings
fall into the pond.
Bossy Bear, Hoppy Rabbit
and Paddy Dog are all afraid.
"What can we do?
The three little ducklings
cannot swim," they say.

"You are silly!" says
Dilly Duck.
"You must know that all little
ducklings can swim."
She hops into the pond too.
Off they go.
Dilly Duck goes first and the
three little ducklings swim
behind her. Silly Dilly Duck
is not so silly after all!

Say these words again

thinks	plays
afraid	roller-skates
first	drives
jumps	second
duckling	funny
swim	scooter
trick	third

What are they doing?

skating

jumping

falling

driving

swimming

PADDY DOG sees a GHOST

Paddy Dog is in his little house. It is a very windy day. Paddy looks out of the window. He sees the leaves falling off the trees.
"It is a good day for doing some washing," he says.
Paddy Dog likes to be clean.

Paddy goes to get all his
dirty washing.
"My sheets are dirty," he says
"and my pillow case too."
Paddy takes the table cloth.
He takes his scarf and his
dirty socks. He puts all the
dirty things into the wash tub.

Then Paddy Dog fills the wash
tub with very hot water.
He puts in lots of soap powder
Then he rubs and he scrubs
until his things are clean.
Paddy goes outside to hang
the clean things on the line.
The wind is blowing hard.

"Now I will go and see Dilly
Duck," says Paddy Dog.
He goes to the duck pond.
Dilly is washing her three
little ducklings.
"It is a good day for doing
washing," says Paddy Dog.
"You are silly!" says Dilly.
"The wind is blowing too hard
Look! All your washing is
blowing away."

"Oh no!" says Paddy Dog. He runs down the lane after his washing. He finds his socks in the hedge. He finds his table cloth on a bush. Flippy Frog finds the scarf and pillow case. They are in the pond.

Poor Paddy Dog.
His washing is all dirty.
He cannot find his sheet.
It is not in the hedge.
It is not in the bush.
It is not by the duck pond.
Is it in the forest?

It is very dark in the forest.
Paddy Dog is afraid.
Something goes "Hoo-hoo-hoo!"
Paddy sees something white.
It is up in the tree.
"A ghost!" says Paddy Dog.
He is not very brave.
Paddy Dog runs away fast.

Paddy runs to Hoppy Rabbit's house. Hoppy is outside, washing his little car.
He rubs and he scrubs until it is clean.
"There is a ghost in the forest!" says Paddy.
"No," says Hoppy Rabbit.
"Yes," says Paddy. "It is up in the tree."
"Let us tell Bossy Bear," says Hoppy Rabbit.

They run to Bossy Bear's
house. Bossy is outside,
washing the windows.
He rubs and he scrubs until
they are clean.
"There is a ghost in the
forest!" say Hoppy and Paddy.
"No," says Bossy.
"Yes," say Hoppy and Paddy.
"It is up in the tree."
"Let us tell Dilly Duck,"
says Bossy.

Dilly and her ducklings are
by the duck pond. Merry Mole
and Flippy Frog are there too.
"There is a ghost in the
forest!" say Paddy and Hoppy
and Bossy.
"You are silly!" says Dilly.
"Come and see," says Paddy
Dog.

So they all go to the forest.
They are afraid, but they
try to be brave.
Then they see something
white in the tree.
"Hoo-hoo-hoo!" it goes.
They all hear it.
"It is a ghost!" says Dilly.
They are not brave at all.
They run away.

Then Cuddly Cat comes by.
She sees something white.
"Hoo-hoo-hoo!" it goes.
"What is that?" says Cuddly.
"It is a ghost in the tree,"
says Paddy Dog.
"I will go and see," says
Cuddly Cat.
"Look out!" says Hoppy.
"The ghost will get you!"

But Cuddly is very brave.
She goes up in the tree.
She lifts up part of the sheet.
"Hoo-hoo-hoo!"
"Look!" says Cuddly Cat.
They all shout,
"We know you!"
It is not a ghost.
It is Ozzie Owl!

Say these words again

windy	clean
blowing	shout
washing	pillow
window	soap powder
outside	something

What can you see?

tub

window

ghost

car

tree

HAPPY
HOPPY RABBIT

It is Hoppy Rabbit's birthday.
He puts out all the things
for his birthday party.
He finds a cloth to put
on the table. He puts the
food on the table too. There
are lots of good things
to eat.

All Hoppy's friends come
to the party. Paddy Dog and
Bossy Bear come first.
"Happy Birthday, Hoppy!"
they say.
"Here is a present for you,"
says Paddy. He gives Hoppy
a big red ball.
"Thank you," says Hoppy,
"I like to play games with
a ball."

Bossy Bear has a present for
Hoppy too.
"Oh, look. It is a kite!"
says Hoppy.
"Look, here come Merry Mole
and Flippy Frog," says Bossy.
"Happy Birthday, Hoppy," they
say. Flippy gives Hoppy a big
bunch of flowers.
"I like flowers," says Hoppy.

Merry Mole has some carrots
for Hoppy.
"I like eating carrots,"
he says. "Thank you."
Then Cuddly Cat comes with
a big basket.
"Thank you," says Hoppy.
He puts all his presents
into the basket.

Here comes Dilly Duck with her three little ducklings. She has made a birthday cake for Hoppy. The ducklings give him lots and lots of big balloons. Hoppy is very happy with all his birthday presents.

"Time to eat!" says Hoppy.
They all go to the table
and they begin to eat.
They eat and they eat until
all the food is gone.
"I like birthdays," says
Hoppy. "Time to play some
games now."

They go outside to play with the big red ball. Hoppy throws it to Paddy. He throws it high into the air. The others try to catch it. They jump up high, but no one can get the ball. Then Cuddly Cat jumps up on to the fence. Now she can catch it.

"This is a very good game!" says Cuddly.

The wind begins to blow.
"Good!" says Hoppy. "Now
I can play with my kite."
He gets the red and blue kite
and he begins to run. The
wind is blowing hard, and
the kite goes up in the air.
"Look at it fly!" says
Bossy Bear.

"Let me have a go," says Paddy.
The kite goes up in the air.
"Let me have a go," says Dilly.
She begins to run, but she does not see Flippy Frog.
BUMP!
She falls over poor Flippy.
Silly Dilly Duck!

Dilly lets go of the kite and it goes up into the air. "Oh no!" they all say. Hoppy, Paddy and Bossy jump up to catch it. But it is stuck high up in the tree. They cannot get it.

Poor Hoppy Rabbit.
He is not very happy now.
"Look!" says Bossy. "I can
get it for you."
Bossy gets up into the tree.
He gets the kite and he begins
to come down.

Then Bossy stops.
"Oh no!" he says.
"I am stuck!"
Bossy cannot get down.
"What can we do?" says Dilly.
"Look!" says Hoppy. He runs
to get all the balloons.
Then he gets the basket.
He ties the balloons to the
basket. Then he lets it go.

Up goes the basket!
It goes up into the tree.
"Get in, Bossy!" says Hoppy.
So Bossy gets into the basket
and it begins to come down.
Down and down it comes.
BUMP!
The basket is down,
Bossy is down,
and the kite is down too!
"What a happy birthday!"
says happy Hoppy Rabbit.

Say these words again

cloth	outside
friends	air
food	throws
eat	catch
first	jumps
present	wind
games	stuck